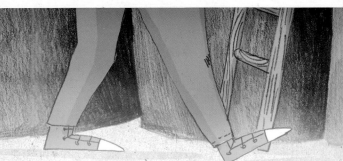

First published 2014 by Walker Books Ltd
87 Vauxhall Walk, London SE11 5HJ

2 4 6 8 10 9 7 5 3 1

Text © 2014 William Bee   Illustrations © 2014 Kate Hindley

The right of William Bee and Kate Hindley to be identified as author and illustrator respectively of this work has been asserted by them in accordance with the Copyright, Designs and Patents Act 1988

This book has been typeset in Aunt Mildred

Printed in China

British Library Cataloguing in Publication Data:
a catalogue record for this book is available from the British Library

ISBN 978-1-4063-3869-0

www.walker.co.uk

OINKINGHAM TV

WITH SPECIAL THANKS TO
AUDREY, OUR ART DIRECTOR,
AND OUR EDITORS, MARIA
AND MANDY.

WORST
IN
SHOW

written by

illustrated by

William Bee

Kate Hindley

WALKER BOOKS
AND SUBSIDIARIES
LONDON · BOSTON · SYDNEY · AUCKLAND

This
is Albert.

And this is Albert's pet monster – Sidney.

Albert thinks Sidney is the best
pet monster in the world.

And today, Albert is going to prove it.
Albert is entering
Sidney in ...

TELEVISION
THEATRE

NO
LITTERING

There are five rounds in
THE BEST PET MONSTER IN THE WORLD!
competition and the pet monster
who receives the most points
overall – wins.

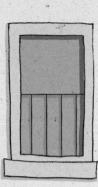

B.P.M.I.T.W.

B.P.M.I.T.W.
PROGRAMME

P.M.I.T.W.
RAMME

ROUND 1
HAIRIEST WARTS

The judges clamber all over the monsters with their measuring devices and the monsters puff themselves up to show off their B I G,

colourful,

h a i r y WARTS.

Goodness the SIZE!

The HAIRS!

OINKINGHAM TV

The JUDGES!
One faints and another
comes out in a rash...

Sidney has done his best.

But Sidney, who has a bath every other day
with lots of soap and bubbles hasn't got any warts —
just a few freckles...

SILENCE
IN THE WINGS

4 50M

GOODNESS
the EMBARRASSMENT!
thinks Albert.

Still, only round one — and who wants a big, HAIRY,
WARTY pet monster anyway?

ROUND 2
HIGHEST HOVER

Everybody has moved outside to see how high the monsters can hover. The judges use hot air balloons and very long tape measures to measure the monsters' hovering height. Goodness the HEIGHT!

The WIND!

50M

7

30M

THE BEST
IN TH
COMP

40M

OINKINGHAM TV

5

8

MONSTER
RLD!
ION

The JUDGES!
One faints and another
floats away in her
untethered balloon...

Sidney has done his best.

But Sidney is scared of heights.
So Sidney hovers very near the ground, so near the ground
in fact that his feet are still touching it...

0 CM

GOODNESS
the EMBARRASSMENT!
thinks Albert.

Still, only round two — and who wants a pet monster
hovering around all day, BUMPING into things anyway?

ROUND 3
MOST PARASITES

Some of the pet monsters have so many parasites that the judges have had to ask the parasites to get off their monsters and line up to be counted.

Goodness the NUMBERS!

The VARIETY!

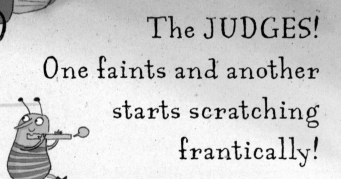

ENTER HERE

NO JUMPING!

QUEUE THIS WAY

The JUDGES!
One faints and another
starts scratching
frantically!

Sidney has done his best.

But Sidney only has two parasites — Stan and Ollie.
And as Stan and Ollie are just staying for a few days ...
they are really holidaymakers rather than parasites.

GOODNESS
the EMBARRASSMENT!
thinks Albert.

Still, only round three — and who wants a
pet monster with hundreds of parasites hanging about
causing all sorts of MISCHIEF anyway?

ROUND 4
SMELLIEST FART

The monsters all position themselves, and on the count of three ... they all FART!

Goodness the SMELL!

The NOISE!

OINKINGHAM TV

FARTOMETER

PONGY!   ROTTEN!

STINKY!   WHIFFY!

STENCHY!   PERFUMEY?

The JUDGES!
One faints and another
runs off holding his nose!

Sidney has done his best.

But a diet of iced biscuits and fairy cakes
means barely a whiff —
and a sugary whiff at that ...

GOODNESS
the EMBARRASSMENT!
thinks Albert.

Still, only round four — and who wants a big SMELLY
pet monster anyway?

It's the final round.

ROUND 5
HOTTEST BREATH

There is chaos onstage!
The monsters take in great
big gulps of air and breathe
out great big bellows of fire!
One of the TV cameras
catches alight and so
do the curtains!

Goodness
   the HEAT!

The SMOKE!

The JUDGES!
One faints and another
runs away holding
her hot bottom!

Sidney has done his best.

But he has only been able to warm up a party sausage
that Albert has put on a little fork...

GOODNESS
the EMBARRASSMENT!
thinks Albert, forlornly.

FIRE
FIRE
FIRE

Still, who wants their BOTTOM
set on fire anyway?

After all the day's excitement, at last —
it's time for the prize giving!

Albert and Sidney wait in
eager anticipation as the
dignitaries hand out
the trophies.

HAIRIEST
WARTS

MOST
PARASITES

HIGHEST
HOVER

Best in Show

SMELLIEST FARTS

But as trophy after trophy is presented to the other pet monsters, it becomes apparent to Albert and Sidney that they are not amongst the winners. GOODNESS the EMBARRASSMENT!

But wait!

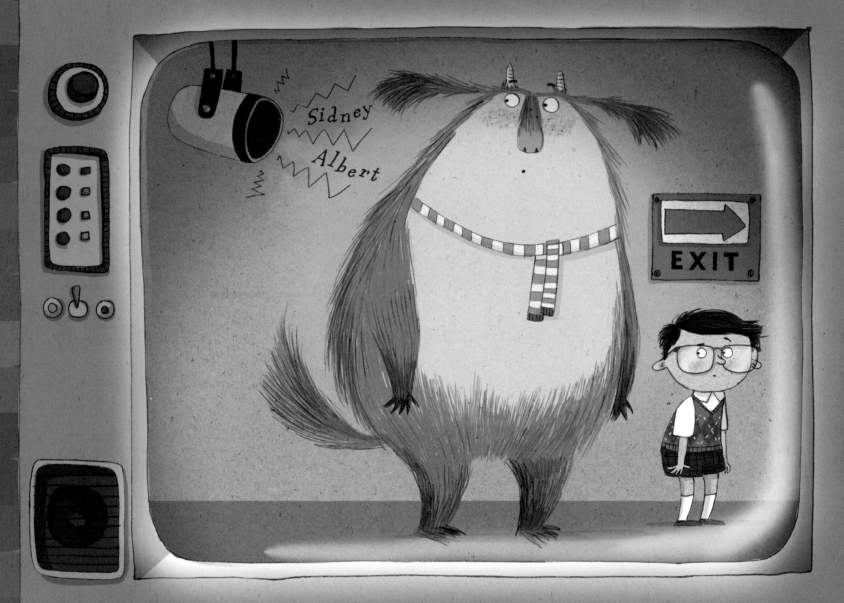

Albert and Sidney's names are being called out!
Winners after all?

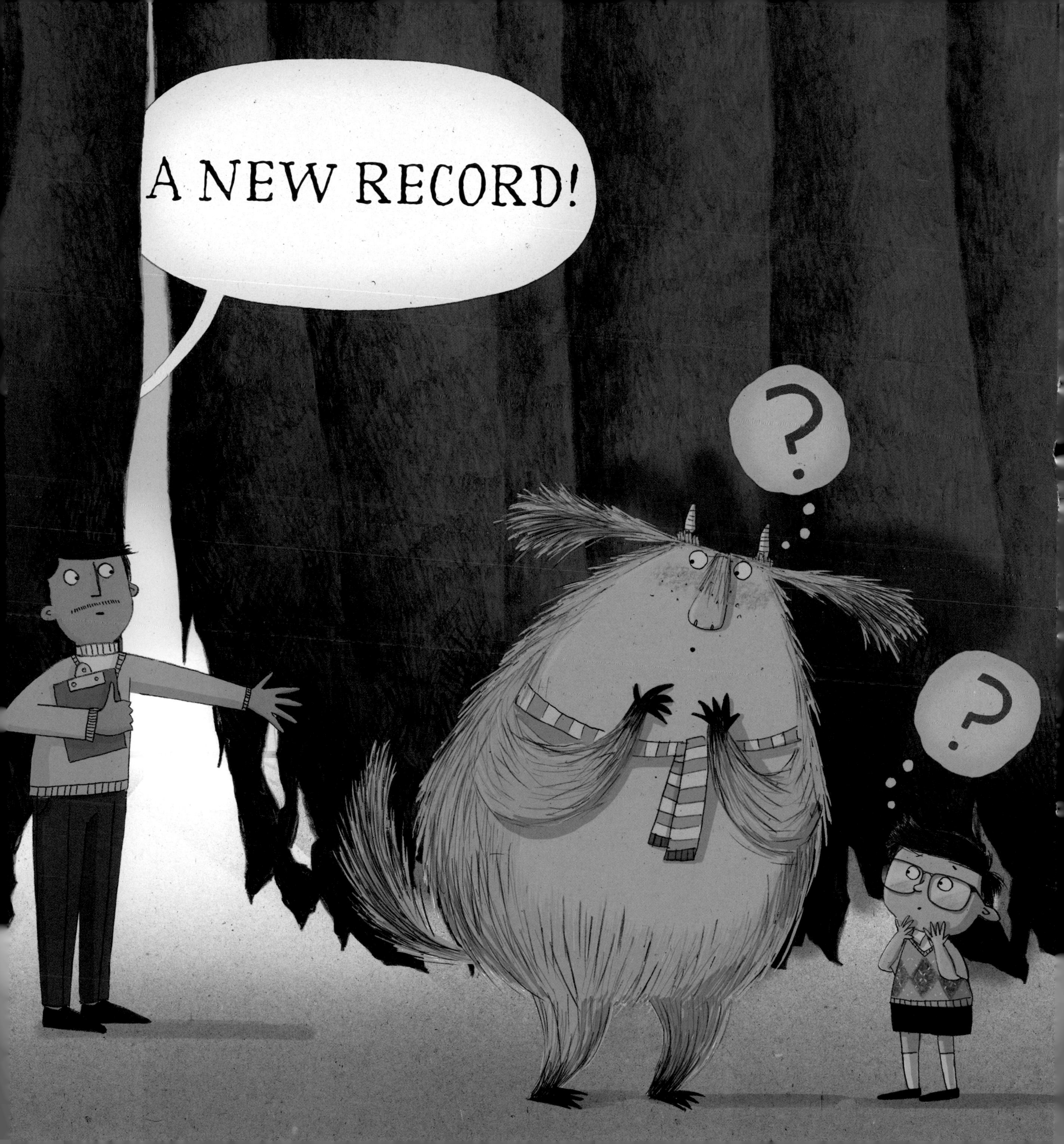
A NEW RECORD!
?
?

The lowest score in one hundred years! Pathetic sugary farts! Freckles instead of warts! Lukewarm party sausages! Zero for hovering! And two comical holiday-makers instead of parasites!

Worst in Show!

GOODNESS the EMBARRASSMENT!
Still, thinks Albert, who wants a big, HAIRY,
HIGH-FLYING, PARASITE-INFESTED,
SMELLY, FLAMMABLE,
pet monster ANYWAY?!

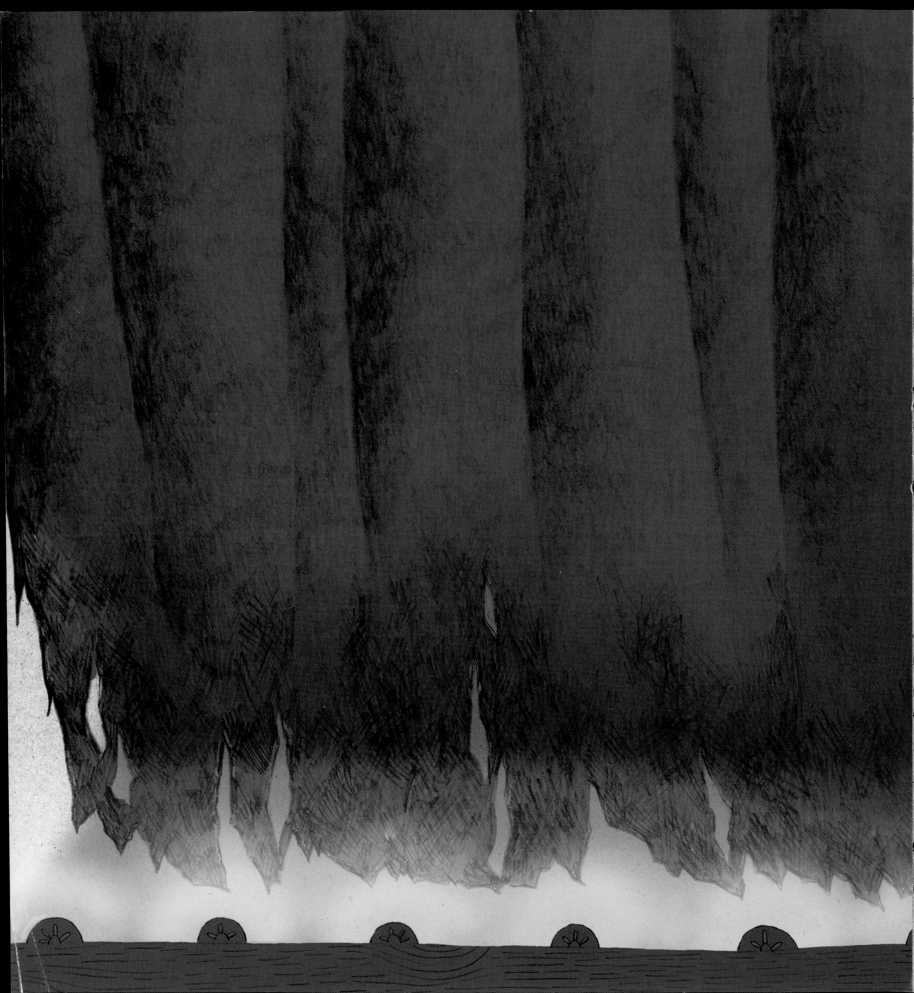

Especially when you can have a
BIG, CUDDLY, LOVABLE . . .
BEST FRIEND.*

*(Who smells GREAT!)

HOME